MOJANG

MINECRAFT
CATCH THE
CREEPER
AND OTHER MOBS

Random House 🏠 New York

Written by Stephanie Milton & Thomas McBrien
Illustrated by Mr. Misang Edited by Thomas McBrien
Designed by John Stuckey, Andrea Philpots, and Jessica Coomber
Special thanks to Alex Wiltshire, Jennifer Hammervald, Kelsey Howard,
Sherin Kwan, Åsa Skogström, Filip Thoms, and Amanda Ström

Original English language edition first published in 2020 under the title *Minecraft Catch the Creeper and Other Mobs: A Search and Find Adventure* by Egmont UK Limited, 2 Minster Court, London EC3R 7BB, United Kingdom.
rhcbooks.com
minecraft.net
ISBN 978-0-593-17312-1
Printed in the United States of America
10 9 8 7 6 5 4 3 2

LOCATIONS

Set out on an adventure across the realm to aid five explorers as they hunt down elusive mobs. The hunt is not going well, and they're in desperate need of your help. Join each explorer as they embark on their quest.

Keep your wits about you! Before the searh is over, you'll need to find elusive wolves, quick-footed white rabbits, and other pesky mobs. Can you help the explorers in their hour of need?

CATCH THE CREEPER

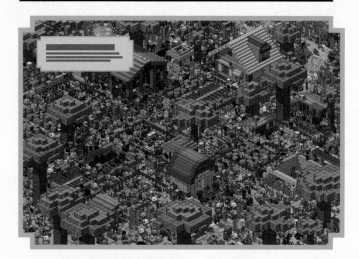

CREEPER ON THE FARM

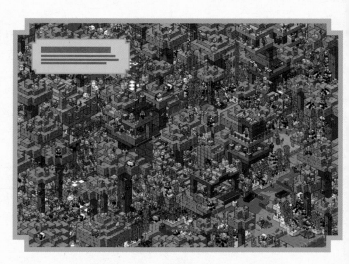

CREEPER IN THE JUNGLE

WHERE'S THE WOLF?

WOLF IN THE TAIGA

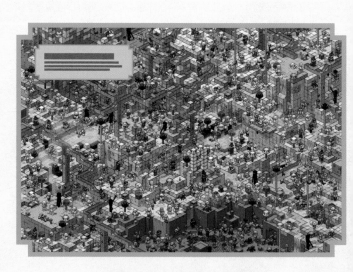

WOLF IN THE CAVES

FOLLOW THE WHITE RABBIT

RABBIT IN THE SNOWY TUNDRA

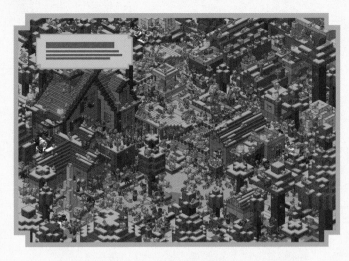

RABBIT IN THE SNOWY TAIGA

SPOT THE WITCH

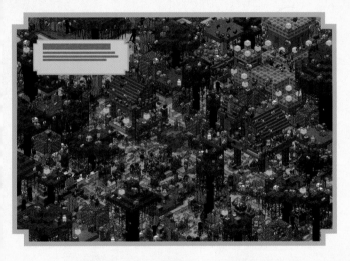

WITCH IN THE SWAMP

WITCH IN THE PLAINS

FIND THE ENDERMAN

ENDERMAN IN THE NETHER

ENDERMAN IN THE END

CATCH
THE CREEPER

Felix and his cats are quite
the adventurers!

They're heading out to explore a dark
forest and a jungle in search of some
fresh supplies. But Felix had better
watch out! There are troublesome
mobs hiding among the trees, waiting to
surprise him. Help him search and find
the mobs in each biome before
they spot him!

FELIX

Meet Felix, a brave explorer who likes to go on adventures with his three cats. Today, Felix is on a mission to catch a creeper so that he can get his hands on the gunpowder he needs to make splash potions. But Felix has forgotten one very important fact: creepers are TERRIFIED of cats and will run away from them as quickly as their short legs can carry them. Felix needs your help to catch the creeper—leaving his cats at home is not an option!

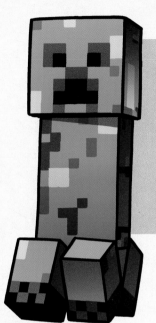

THE CREEPER

Here's the creeper that Felix is trying to catch. On a normal day it would be creeping around very quietly, trying to find an explorer to explode. Today, however, it's on the run from Felix's cats. If Felix manages to catch and defeat it, it will drop gunpowder. **THE CHASE IS ON!**

THE ARMORED ZOMBIE

This is a rare and terrifying sight—an armored zombie! Without a helmet, zombies will burn in the sun, but with a helmet, they can happily shamble around in broad daylight. This dangerous zombie is on the prowl, wandering around searching for unsuspecting players to terrorize.

THE DROWNED

Drowned mobs are usually found lurking underwater, but sometimes they climb up onto dry land to give adventurers a fright. There's nothing they enjoy more than terrorizing explorers—sometimes they're armed with tridents, which they will throw at their target. This drowned mob has Felix fixed in its sights and is in hot pursuit! RAAAAAUUGGGGHHH!

THE TURTLE

Turtles love to swim in the ocean. No matter how far from home a turtle travels, it will always find its way back to the beach where it spawned. This turtle is trying to find its way home but has gotten a little lost. Can you see where it disappeared to?

CREEPER ON THE FARM

Felix has tracked the creeper to this farm! Somehow the creeper and other mobs have managed to sneak in. Quick, track them down before they cause any mayhem!

ABSOLUTELY

NO

CREEPERS

CREEPER IN THE JUNGLE

The mobs have hhngle. Felix and his feline friends are in pursuit! Round them up before they can get away again.

WHERE'S THE WOLF?

Scarlett has set out
into the wild in search
of new biomes.

She has found a rich new taiga biome
and can't wait to explore the area.
Alas, she has lost her pet wolf! The sun
is setting quickly, and mobs are starting
to emerge. Help Scarlett spot the
dangerous mobs while she searches
for her missing companion.

SCARLETT

This is Scarlett. Scarlett spends her time searching for new biomes and rare treasures. She has a wolf called Luna, who goes with her on all her expeditions. Most of the time, Scarlett and Luna are inseparable, but Scarlett can be a little forgetful—she sometimes makes Luna sit while she goes off to do something extra dangerous, then forgets where she left her wolf. Keep an eye out for Scarlett as she sets off on her adventure.

LUNA

Luna used to live in a dark forest with lots of other wolves. One day, Scarlett found Luna and fed her a juicy bone. Now Luna goes everywhere Scarlett goes—unless Scarlett tells her to sit, of course. Luna has a blue collar and likes to chase skeletons.

THE BLACK CAT

You're sure to see a lot of cats when you go exploring, especially if you find a village. There are many different cat breeds, and they have many different markings. But there's only one black cat prowling around. It's probably on the hunt for some delicious fish.

THE SPIDER JOCKEY

Now, here's a sight you don't see every day—a skeleton riding a spider! That doesn't look very comfortable. This horrifying beast has the speed of a spider and the strength of a skeleton—eek!

THE CAVE SPIDER

These poisonous dark blue spiders live in abandoned mineshafts deep underground, but sometimes they find their way to the surface. They can climb steep walls and fit into tight spaces. You don't want to get into a fight with a cave spider—a single bite will quickly sap your health bar!

WOLF IN THE TAIGA

Scarlett has left Luna sitting somewhere in this taiga biome. Alas, Scarlett can't remember where she last saw her! And with so many wolves, she's having a hard time finding Luna again.

WOLF IN THE CAVES

Luna is sitting patiently somewhere in these caves, waiting for Scarlett to return with a pocket full of shiny diamonds. Luna has been waiting a long time. What a well-behaved wolf!

FOLLOW THE WHITE RABBIT

Brrrrr, it's cold!

Max has trekked through biomes for days, only to find himself lost in tundra and knee-deep in snow. There's no way he's going to stay here! He's going to set off toward a warmer climate just as soon as he gathers enough supplies. All he needs is a white rabbit's foot, but all the white snow is making it difficult to find anything. Will you help Max?

MAX

Max is irritated. He has lost his map and wandered into a cold and snowy tundra biome, when he'd much prefer to be on a sunny beach by the water. It looks like Max is in for a long journey in search of a warmer climate, so he's decided to stock up on potions of leaping to speed things up a bit. He needs to get his hands on some rabbits' feet. Luckily, he knows that where there's snow, there are also white rabbits. The search is on!

THE WHITE RABBIT

This white rabbit is extremely good at hiding in snowy biomes—its fur helps it blend in with the environment, making it very hard to spot. It can run fast, so it's difficult to catch as well. If Max manages to catch and defeat it, it might drop the rabbit's foot he needs. The white rabbit may look similar to the killer bunny, but they're not related!

THE SNOW GOLEM

Max has made himself a snow golem to help keep dangerous mobs at bay. Crafted from two blocks of snow and a carved pumpkin, it provides some welcome companionship in this lonely biome. The snow golem likes to wander around pelting snowballs at unsuspecting mobs.

THE CHICKEN JOCKEY

A baby zombie riding a chicken? This is almost as bad as the spider jockey! Chicken jockeys are extremely hostile. They can move quickly and fit through very small gaps. Unfortunately for Max, one of their favorite pastimes is terrorizing explorers. Warning: Do NOT try to feed this chicken any seeds!

THE POLAR BEAR

If you keep your eyes peeled, you'll occasionally see a polar bear plodding through the snow. If you're lucky, you may even see a whole family of them together. Max has never seen a polar bear, and he is determined to catch a glimpse of one before he leaves this snowy biome. He knows not to step near their precious cubs.

RABBIT IN THE SNOWY TUNDRA

The white rabbit was last seen hopping through this vast snowy tundra biome. Small white creatures are very difficult to spot here, so Max needs some help!

RABBIT IN THE SNOWY TAIGA

The chase continues—the quick-footed white rabbit ran off into a neighboring snowy taiga before Max could grab it. Now it's hiding somewhere among the trees.

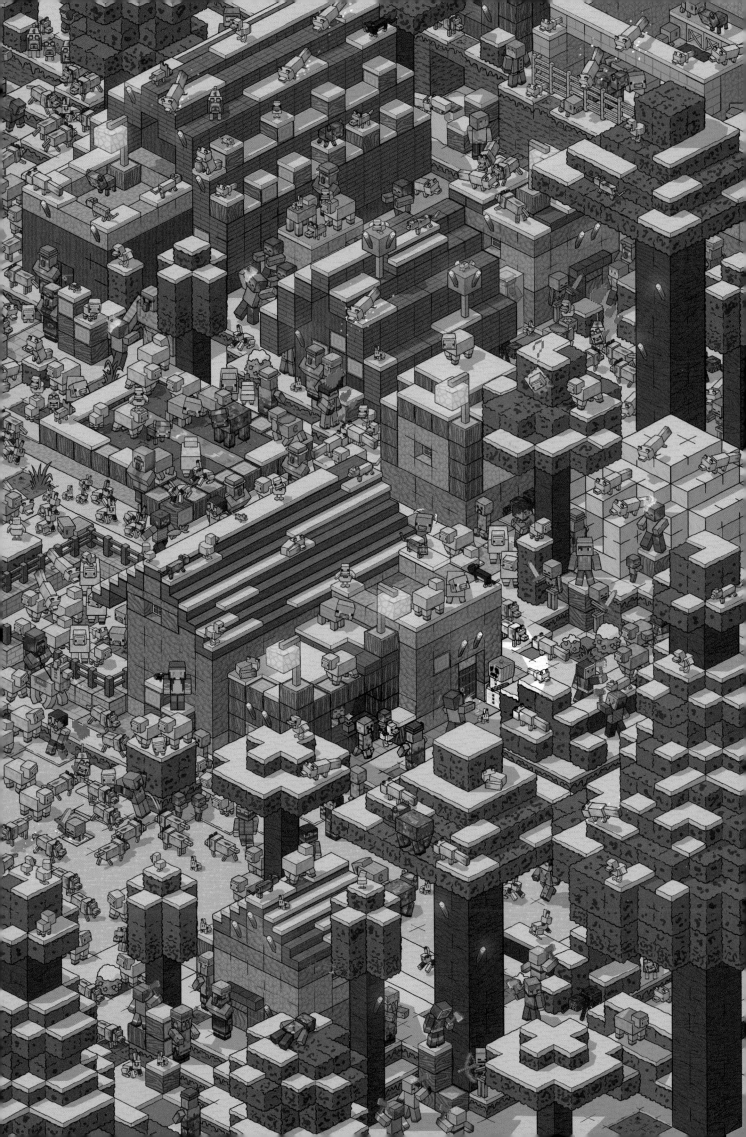

SPOT
THE WITCH

Zoe is on a mission. She wants to find and defeat a witch.

But where in the world can they be found? Zoe has traveled for days without sleep, tracking a witch's trail to a boggy swamp. Help Zoe catch the witch—but look out! It's getting late, and pillagers and phantoms have come out to hassle the adventurer on her quest!

ZOE

Zoe loves exploring the Overworld. The Nether is a bit too dangerous for her liking! She's always wanted a glowstone lamp for her house, though, and everyone knows that glowstone is found in the Nether. Fortunately for Zoe, witches sometimes drop glowstone dust when they're defeated, so she might not have to brave the Nether after all. Zoe has decided track down and defeat a witch. Hopefully it will drop the glowstone she has always wanted.

THE WITCH

This witch has been causing an awful lot of trouble recently. When it's not throwing harmful splash potions at unsuspecting explorers, it's raiding villages or scaring miners in caves. Zoe will be doing everyone a favor if she manages to defeat it—but only if she can find it first!

THE PILLAGER

This crossbow-wielding maniac targets explorers, villagers, and iron golems without mercy. Sometimes it accidentally hits a hostile mob with its arrows, too, which can be fun to watch. Rumor has it a pillager has been spotted nearby.

THE RAVAGER

These enormous beasts join pillagers raiding villages. Like pillagers, they are hostile toward explorers, villagers, and iron golems. They use their head to ram their opponents, causing extreme damage. Make sure you don't get trampled by this mob!

THE PHANTOM

This undead, airborne horror swoops down from the skies and attacks explorers who haven't slept in a few days. It's only ever seen at night—phantoms burn in the sunlight, just like zombies and other undead mobs. Zoe is desperate to avoid the phantom if she can, but she hasn't slept in days and knows it's out there waiting for her.

WITCH IN THE SWAMP

The witch has returned to its native swamp for the night. Let's hope nobody has moved into its hut or they're in for a nasty shock—witches do not like to share.

WITCH IN THE PLAINS

The sun is about to rise, and the witch has made its way to a nearby plains biome. It must be planning to terrorize the peaceful villagers and make off with their valuables.

FIND THE ENDERMAN

Oliver, the renowned knight of the realm, has set out to defeat every mob in Minecraft.

He has struck down a mighty pillager, slain an undead skeleton, and even bested a three-headed wither! Along with his trusty steed, Turbo, Oliver is set to travel the land until he has defeated them all. Only a few remain; will you help him on his quest?

OLIVER

Oliver has defeated every dangerous mob in the Overworld and the Nether. Now he's ready to visit the End and face his final challenge: the vicious ender dragon! He has found a stronghold, but he needs one more ender pearl to activate the End portal. Oliver can't find any endermen in the Overworld, so he's going to try his luck in the Nether. One ender pearl is all that stands between him and greatness! Oh, and the ender dragon, of course.

THE ENDERMAN

Endermen are mysterious creatures. Tall, thin, and black as night, they make strange, otherworldly noises and teleport around aimlessly. They're also known to pick up blocks and move them around. If you make eye contact, an enderman will become hostile and attack you. Oliver needs to slay one to get the missing ender pearl. Watch out—only target the hostile enderman!

THE WITHER

The wither is one of Minecraft's most dangerous mobs. It shoots explosive skulls at its target and is immune to fire, lava, and drowning. Oliver is famous for summoning the wither wherever he goes. It provides him with a nether star so he can craft a beacon, and also lets him practice his latest combat moves. Hiiiiii-yah!

THE IRON GOLEM

This giant utility mob can be an adventurer's best friend. It will attack dangerous mobs as soon as it sees them. Like many explorers, Oliver likes to craft an iron golem whenever he finds himself in a dangerous environment so he has an ally to help him fight off hostile mobs. Iron golems are particularly good at helping the undead return to the grave.

TURBO

Turbo is Oliver's loyal companion and the fastest horse in Minecraft. He never goes anywhere without Oliver. Turbo is easily spooked, but Oliver always manages to coax him through the Nether portal, even if he has to bribe him with some golden carrots.

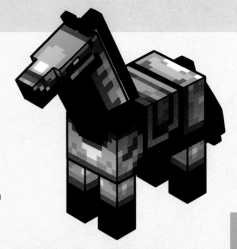

ENDERMAN IN THE NETHER

The Nether is crawling with dangerous mobs, so there must be an enderman around here somewhere. Oliver knows they are found in Soul Sand valley. He's on a mission to find one.

ENDERMAN IN THE END

Oliver has found the last ender pearl he needed to activate the End portal! He has invited all his friends to enter the portal and watch as he defeats his final adversary.

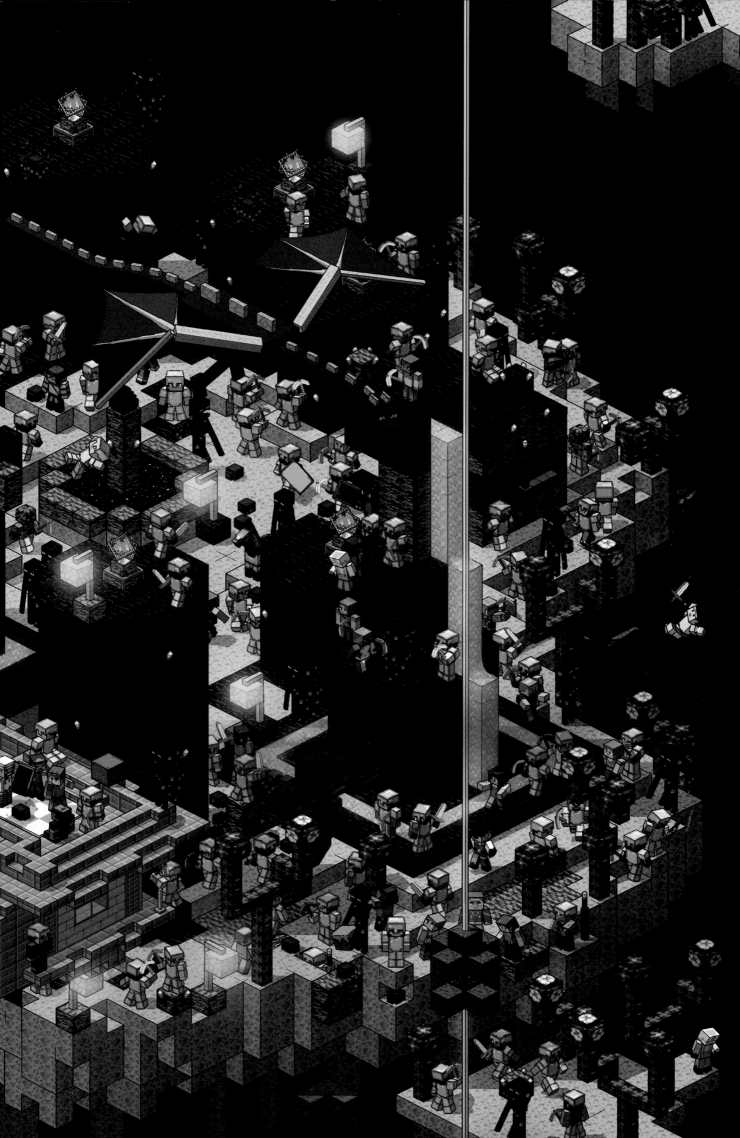

WHAT ELSE CAN YOU FIND?

Congratulations! Thanks to your efforts, our brave adventurers have gone about their quest with great success.

You must be a natural explorer, to have made it this far unscathed! Are you ready for another challenge? We've heard some wild rumors lately, and we want you to see if you can verify them. Retrace your steps and see if you can find all these bonus items.

CREEPER ON THE FARM

- [ ] A witch pretending to be a scarecrow
- [ ] An upside-down sheep
- [ ] A pig with a bucket on its head
- [ ] A chicken digging an escape tunnel
- [ ] A pig eating a piece of cake
- [ ] A villager taking photos of the farm

CREEPER IN THE JUNGLE

- [ ] Parrots dancing around a jukebox
- [ ] A house made from melon blocks
- [ ] A panda with a slice of cake
- [ ] A player about to trip a tripwire
- [ ] A creeper statue
- [ ] A pig with a cookie

WOLF IN THE TAIGA

- [ ] A creeper peering out a window
- [ ] Two wolves fighting over cooked chicken
- [ ] Wolves chasing a player holding a steak
- [ ] A killer bunny
- [ ] A player falling out of a tree
- [ ] A chicken riding on a wolf's back

WOLF IN THE CAVES

- [ ] An exploding creeper
- [ ] A zombie stuck in cobwebs
- [ ] A player searching for ores with a metal detector
- [ ] Two players fighting over an emerald
- [ ] A skeleton taking a nap
- [ ] An enderman mining with a pickaxe

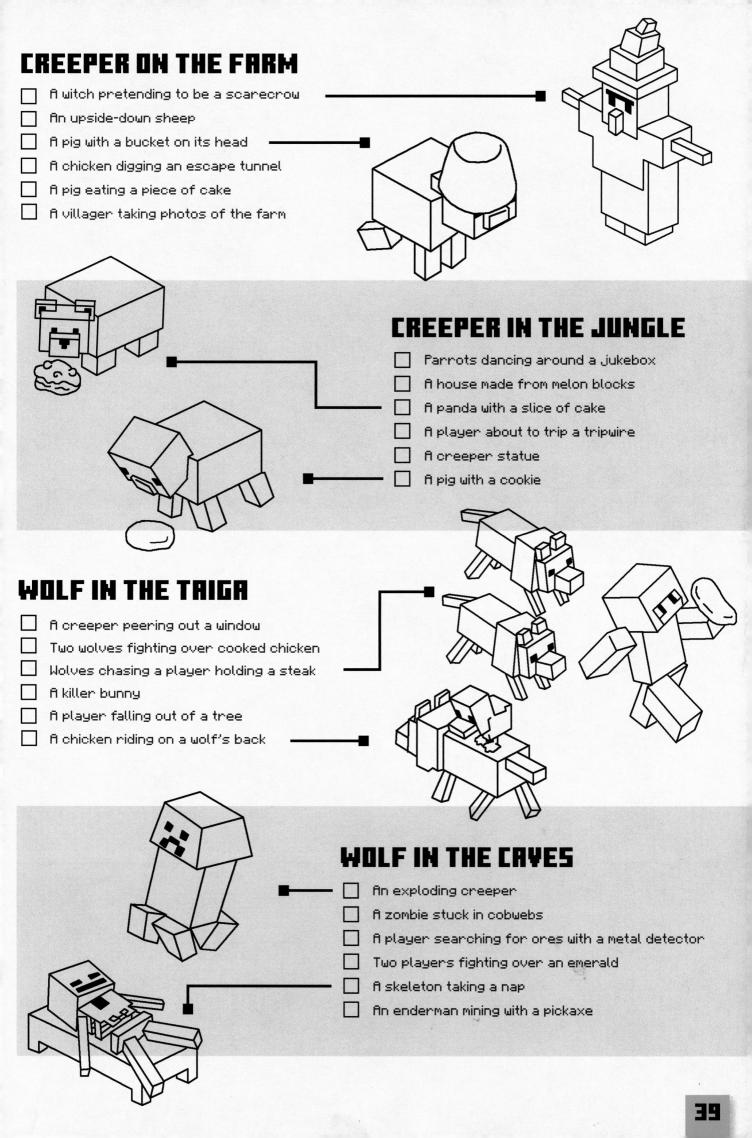

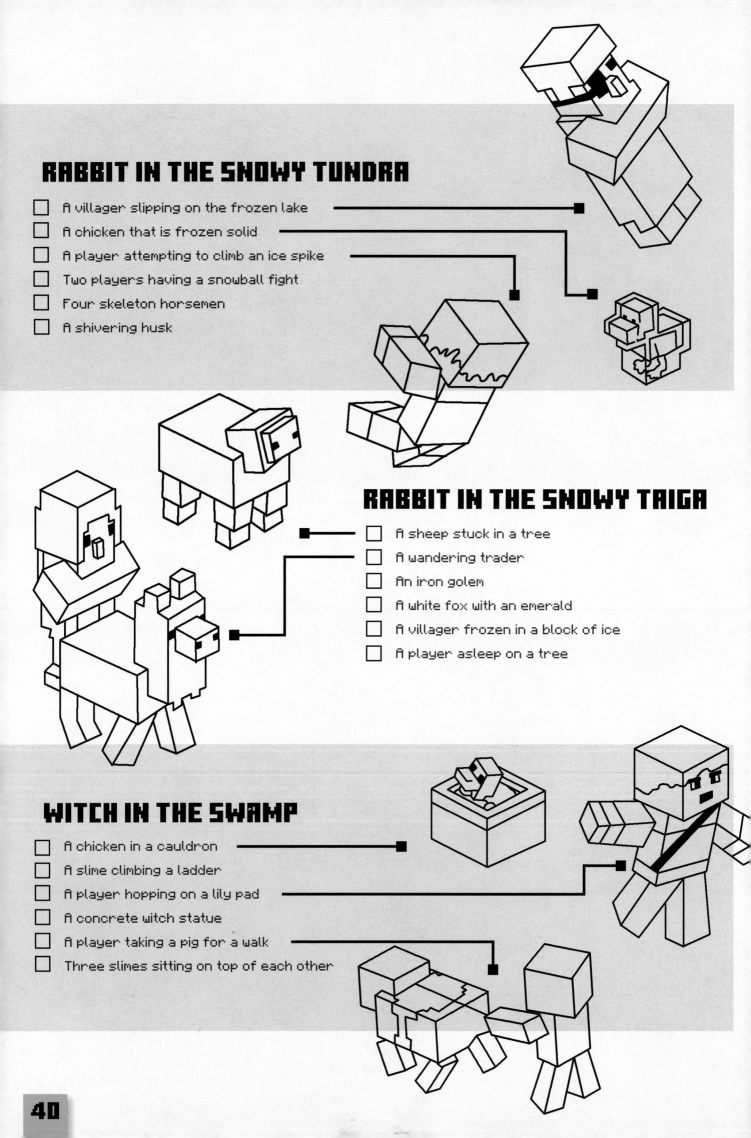

RABBIT IN THE SNOWY TUNDRA

- [ ] A villager slipping on the frozen lake
- [ ] A chicken that is frozen solid
- [ ] A player attempting to climb an ice spike
- [ ] Two players having a snowball fight
- [ ] Four skeleton horsemen
- [ ] A shivering husk

RABBIT IN THE SNOWY TAIGA

- [ ] A sheep stuck in a tree
- [ ] A wandering trader
- [ ] An iron golem
- [ ] A white fox with an emerald
- [ ] A villager frozen in a block of ice
- [ ] A player asleep on a tree

WITCH IN THE SWAMP

- [ ] A chicken in a cauldron
- [ ] A slime climbing a ladder
- [ ] A player hopping on a lily pad
- [ ] A concrete witch statue
- [ ] A player taking a pig for a walk
- [ ] Three slimes sitting on top of each other

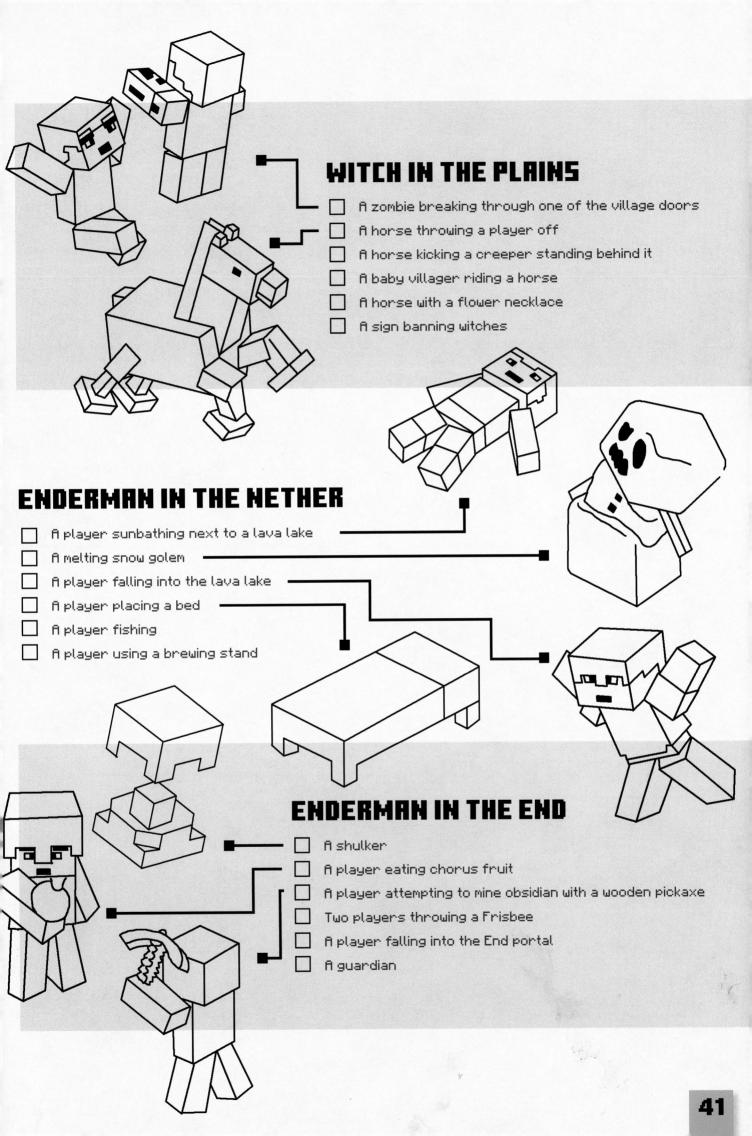

WITCH IN THE PLAINS

- ☐ A zombie breaking through one of the village doors
- ☐ A horse throwing a player off
- ☐ A horse kicking a creeper standing behind it
- ☐ A baby villager riding a horse
- ☐ A horse with a flower necklace
- ☐ A sign banning witches

ENDERMAN IN THE NETHER

- ☐ A player sunbathing next to a lava lake
- ☐ A melting snow golem
- ☐ A player falling into the lava lake
- ☐ A player placing a bed
- ☐ A player fishing
- ☐ A player using a brewing stand

ENDERMAN IN THE END

- ☐ A shulker
- ☐ A player eating chorus fruit
- ☐ A player attempting to mine obsidian with a wooden pickaxe
- ☐ Two players throwing a Frisbee
- ☐ A player falling into the End portal
- ☐ A guardian

ANSWERS

Your adventure is now complete! Did you find everything? Was the white rabbit too elusive, or did the creeper sneak away? Check the answers for each scene below and find any that you've missed.

KEY: Explorer Quests = **WHITE**   What Else Can You Find? = **RED**

CATCH THE CREEPER

CREEPER ON THE FARM

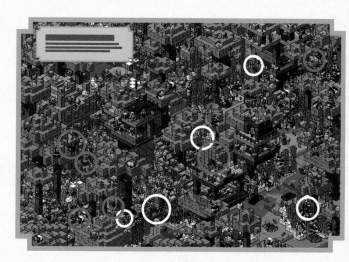

CREEPER IN THE JUNGLE

WHERE'S THE WOLF?

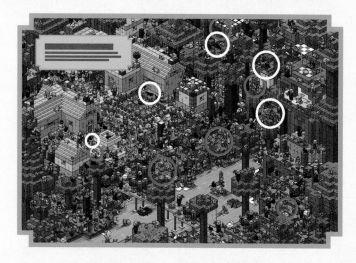

WOLF IN THE TAIGA

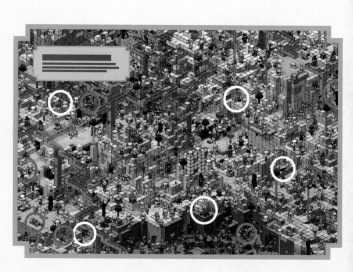

WOLF IN THE CAVES

FOLLOW THE WHITE RABBIT

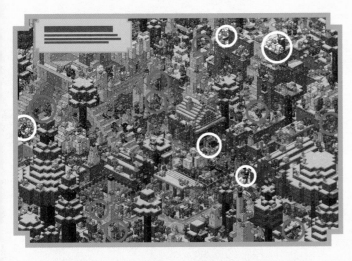

RABBIT IN THE SNOWY TUNDRA

RABBIT IN THE SNOWY TAIGA

SPOT THE WITCH

WITCH IN THE SWAMP

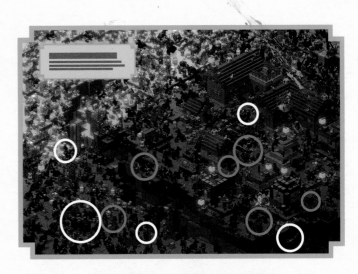

WITCH IN THE PLAINS

FIND THE ENDERMAN

ENDERMAN IN THE NETHER

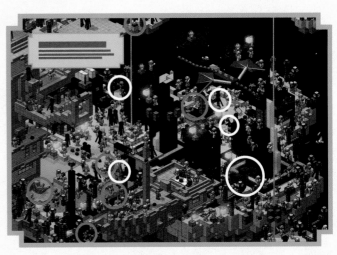

ENDERMAN IN THE END

GOTCHA!